Old
and
New

Acknowledgments
Executive Editor: Diane Sharpe
Supervising Editor: Stephanie Muller
Design Manager: Sharon Golden
Page Design: Simon Balley Design Associates
Photography: The Architectural Association: cover (bottom left), page 15;
Beamish, the North of England Open Air Museum: page 19; Chris Fairclough
Colour Library: page 17 (left); Graco Children's Products: page 25 (bottom);
Robert Harding Picture Library: page 27 (left); Image Bank: page 17 (right);
Last Resort Picture Library: pages 7, 9, 23, 27 (right); The National Motor Museum,
Beaulieu: page 13 (both); Popperfoto: page 25 (top); Alex Ramsay: page 21.

ISBN 0-8114-3719-1

Old and New

Paul Humphrey and
Alex Ramsay

Illustrated by
Sarah Young

STECK-VAUGHN®
C O M P A N Y
ELEMENTARY • SECONDARY • ADULT • LIBRARY

It's about old things
and new things.

5

My new doll walks and talks.

She can even eat baby food!

This old doll is made of
china.

This old toy car can move.

You have to wind it up to make it work.

8

Some new toy cars have
batteries to make them work.

9

Let's look around outside for more old and new things.

12

Old cars look very different
from cars today.

13

These houses are over 100 years old. The buildings behind them are very new.

People's faces change as
they get older.

Look at this old photo.

It's of my grandpa when he was young.

18

People wore very different
clothes when your grandparents
were young.

Oak trees can live for
hundreds of years.

Bikes are painted very
bright colors today.

There's an old baby buggy in here, too.

Mom bought a new stroller for the baby.

24

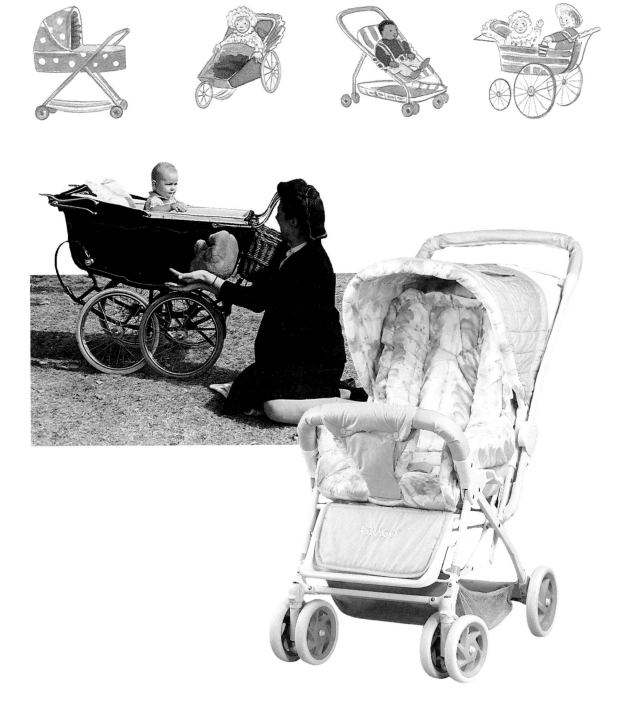

Old baby buggies had big wheels. New strollers have small wheels.

Old leaves are brown and
brittle. New ones are green.

I like new things.

28

But old things
are nice, too.

Some of the things on this page are old, and some are new. Can you tell which ones are which?

Index